Nicollette Gonadu Presents

Wayrotic Stories

Nicollette Gonadu

Thynkupp Publishing Company
New Orleans

Nicollette Gonadu Presents Wayrotic Stories

A Thynkupp Publishing Book

Library Catalogue Card Number:

For information address:
Thynkupp Publishing Company

ISBN 9780996502702

I dedicate this book to my heart Nes, you love me completely, the good, the bad, and the ugly, And It's Still All Good. Friend to Friend Forever.

Acknowledgements

I would first like to thank all of my friends, Rosetta Maddred, Ivy, Morenike, Shannon, Mecca, Paris, Tasha, Aquila, Nuri, Ms. Moon, Nisha, Yolanda, Antoinette, Matuca, Teesh, Sonora, Kelli, Erica, and my two very best friends Navada & Jamillah, for listening, laughing, and not lying. I started writing these stories during my divorce contemplation. I was scared of the dating scene and had planned to find safety in self parties, but life has a way of opening doors and come to find out you get a choice of going in to the ones you want…it's not over until you decide it is. These stories are completely fictional, I wrote them to help relationships renew themselves and also to help single women keep it tight until they find the real Mr. Right. My Editor Lorraine, I can't thank you enough for reading my initial works and giving me great clarity.

Nicollette Gonadu Presents

Wayrotic Stories

Table of Contents

8

Two on One, One Thursday Night

It was three of them this evening, Lillian was nervous because she knew what was going to happen tonight, they had talked about it several times since they first started dating. Lillian was going to let it happen tonight. Lev and Tell were cousins and had been double teaming females since they were in elementary, back then it was just humping and grinding with their clothes on, but when they got to college it was way more involved. The only reason Lillian was different was because she was Lev's girl, his woman, but she had a fantasy and she found Tell very attractive. The two looked similar facially but physique wise they had nothing in common. Lev was brown skinned with a medium build, he was about six feet even, he wore a ceasar cut filled with waves and had the most adorable eyes, sexy and sweet, his body was firm but it wasn't cut with muscles like Tell's. Tell was a physical trainer and all 6'4" of him showed it, his body was ripped, his arms were muscular and his fingers were long and slender, it was safe to assume that there was an eight pack beneath his plaid shirt.

The night was typical, they sat out on the balcony of Lillian's apartment overlooking the city of Atlanta. They were four stories up and had a great view. Lillian's roommate had recently moved out and took most of the furniture with her. The balcony was now the only place with seating besides the bedroom. It was nicely decorated, with plants along side the railing, creating a little privacy from the condos across the street.

They had been drinking, playing music, and eating fresh strawberries from the Farmer's Market since 5 pm, things they had all done before especially this summer in particular. It had been driving Lillian crazy to watch Tell suck on the ice at the bottom of his glass, he would use those long fingers to reach them and the way he would put one in his mouth made Lillian want to be between his lips and on his tongue. Every time she caught herself staring she would try to avert her eyes and look at Lev, but that didn't help much because his lips made her want to french kiss. She sat there drinking her drink feeling herself throb from the closeness of both of them. They were drinking Jameson with club soda on ice and the fifth was getting low. They were laughing louder and louder at Tell's corny jokes, he had a habit of making fun of his clients in a professional tone which made it more hilarious. The breeze was just picking up, and Lillian got up to get a wrap.

"Where are you going Lil?' Tell asked, "You're not trying to slip away are you?"

"Slip where?" said Lil, "I'm just going to get something to wrap around me, it's kind of cold out here."

"Come here baby," Lev grabbed her to his lap and gently kissed her neck, "you won't be cold for long."

He stroked her arms as she sat on his lap with her back facing his chest, slowly his light kisses became wet kisses on her neck and in her ear, Lillian had on a spaghetti strapped sundress, Tell came over and began sliding it up her legs. He only used one finger to move it and with his other hand he traced up her calf to her inner thigh. Lev used his hands to palm her breast, he was kissing her shoulders at the same time. Lillian's eyes were closed and she had the biggest smile on her face as Tell realized that she wasn't wearing any panties.

"Oh girl, you need to stop playing, Lev she is wet as hell," Tell said this as he was sliding his ring finger in and out of her pussy. His dick became hard feeling how slippery Lillian was becoming around his hand, he had to readjust himself and slow his breathing down.

Lillian was one of the sexiest ladies he had ever seen, she was petite and had the most alluring walk, he wasn't sure if it was her ass or her hips that enticed him more, but feeling on her pussy lips was making him want to feel her better with his dick.

She moaned her pleasure, her mind was spinning, their breathing had become hers, her nipples were now exposed and her pussy was being gently fingered, it was all so erotic because it was just as she had imagined, it was slow and sensual. Lillian's entire body was being appreciated by two men at once, and they each knew well what they were doing. Tell saw Lillian biting her lip, he wanted to bite something too.

"Lev put your hand down here on this wet pussy and let me at those nipples," Tell spoke low but he was completely audible. Lillian's head was bursting now because they never took their hands off of her body as they switched positions. Tell placed one breast in his hand and the other gently in his mouth and sucked.

Lillian moaned some more, because as she sat on Lev's lap feeling his hard dick on her ass and lower back, he was gently sliding two fingers in and out of her while his other two rubbed the pearl that had become swollen, Tell squeezed and licked her breasts, he even bit her a few times. It was then that she noticed that her hands were doing nothing, she was only using them to brace herself on the armrest. She raised one hand to Tell's chin pulling him up to her face, his hands tweaked and pulled at her nipples as she kissed him on those soft lips that she could never stop staring at, his tongue found hers but didn't move, she entered him instead.

"Oh baby," she moaned as Lev found her rhythm and began rocking her back and forth, "Oh baby, put it in, please, put it in," Lillian was whispering this in Tell's ear. Her breath was still sweet from the strawberries, and warm against his ear making his dick harder than he thought possible. He wanted her to feel it, he wanted her to know how much she turned him on. He took her hand from his face and placed it on his dick, he kept his hand on top of hers as she stroked it, her other hand went to her mouth so that she could wet her fingers before she began to massage his balls.

Lev lifted her up by her ass and spread her lips with one hand and guided his dick in with the other. Lillian was breathing very hard and deeply and was completely over the edge. A dick in the bush and one in the hand, and Tell had just put a finger in her mouth.

Lillian bent forward and put her mouth on the head

of Tell's penis, he let out a loud breath. "Damn this shit feels good," he said this a little louder than he wanted to.

Lev had his hands on her waist manipulating her body to his rhythm, he was enjoying her enjoying herself and her pussy was getting wetter and wetter around his dick. The deeper she went with Tell's rod in her throat, the tighter her pussy gripped his dick, he started breathing hard. Lev bent forward and began to bite her shoulders and the back of her neck. He whispered in her ear, "Your pussy's so wet right now".

"I know," she moaned back.

Tell was losing control because Lillian was making a lot of sounds with the tip of his dick in her mouth.

Lev was losing it because she was tightening her thighs, which was tightening her pussy up around his penis. She wanted them to both come on her, so she sped up her pace on both of them, she felt them both stiffen, Tell in her mouth and Lev between her legs, they were both feeling good and she knew it. Quickly she jacked Tell's dick and let it spill on her lips and chin, he let out a loud deep groan and fell back against the railing to breathe. Lev was trying to last longer but he couldn't, his nut was at the last edge, Lillian got up off of him and turned around to face him on her knees to receive his come it missed her mouth and shot on her titties, it was so hot, she couldn't believe how much power was behind it. Her body started to shake as an orgasm took hold of her, she had always wanted to feel two men at once and two sexy men was her fantasy come true and from that experience she learned that cum on her body made her have the hardest orgasm ever, she wasn't sure if she would initiate it again, but if Lev offered she would be with it.

The Essence Fest

"Girl this place is so crowded, I hope we can see the stage," Mirah said with an attitude. She and her girlfriend Lynette had just arrived at the Superdome to see the Essence Festival, they had missed all the opening acts and still had to find their seats.

"I'm just glad we ain't miss Mary, cause your late ass would be getting fucked up if I..." Lynette didn't get to finish.

"Girl please, I'm one second off you anyway for that shit you just pulled in the line", Mirah told her.

"What? You didn't even know him," Lynette shot back.

"Exactly, I would have loved to get know his sexy ass," Mirah smiled.

"He was sexy as hell, them eyes was all slitted up, that nigga was high as hell," Lynette laughed at her friend.

"He sure wasn't drunk," Mirah and Lynette both laughed.

"Oh here we go, this is our section," Lynette and Mirah squeezed past a few people to get to their seats.

"Good, I can see perfectly, oh shit there's dude," Mirah couldn't keep the big smile off of her face.

"Where?" Lynette looked ahead.

"Two rows in front of us," Mirah pointed, "when Mary comes on I'm going to go to his section, you coming?"

"No," Lynette told her, "his boys ain't as fine as he is."

"Oh well you know what they say, 'image is nothing'," Mirah said.

"No that's what you say," Lynette said to her girl.

Mary J. Blige came out and began singing *Work That Thing Out*, giving Mirah the courage to go and approach dude, he was standing up at his seat with everyone else enjoying the show, she just walked up in front of him with her back to him and started dancing, he placed his hand on her waist and brought her closer to him.

"Baby how tall are you?" he asked her.

"5'10" with out the high heeled sandals", she replied.

He whispered in her ear, "Baby, you a tree I can't wait to climb."

"What?" she looked back at him and laughed, "Where are you from?"

"Right Chere," he said in a thick New Orleans accent.

"A native, huh? What's your name?" she asked over the music.

"Where are you from?", he asked not answering her question, "I hear some Mid West."

"You right, I'm from St. Louis, and this is my shit," Mary was singing *I Can Love You*.

He was rubbing his hands up and down her sides as she was grinding against him. The whole row of people were dancing and rapping along with Lil Kim's part.

"With your fine ass", he told her.
It was definitely the outfit, Mirah was happy with
what she was wearing, though he was the type that
would fuck through your daisy dukes, she loved that
she had put on her white bustier dress with the
Austrian crystals sprinkled throughout. She had set
her breast higher than normal with the black rose of
her nipples showing. She continued to dance against
him trying to make his dick hard, she was pleased that
he was wearing linen pants that didn't leave much to
the imagination.

He was staring down her front, his chin in her
shoulder, "I see that black rose, yeah," he whispered
in a raspy voice, "go 'head get nasty," he encouraged
her to keep moving like she was, "girl I'm gonna send
you home with a sprung leak, hope you ain't got to
work Monday, I would love to fuck you baby girl."

"Where I'm from we have a saying, "Don't talk
about it, be about it," she threw her head back to
whisper that in his ear. She made sure he got her
meaning by using her middle finger to trace up his
palm.

"Sexy ass," he whispered back, "but baby you can't
take all this dick for the first time right here."

He took his hand slid it up her dress and moved her
panties out of his way and put his fingers on the top
of her pussy, all this was happening while she kept
grinding her ass against his dick. Even though her
pussy was slippery wet he would not enter her, he just
rubbed the hole with his finger. *Someone please call
911.* Mary had the crowd rocking so hard that no one
noticed the couple getting it in. He took her hand,
licked her finger and followed the black rose of her

breast with it.

"Baby you sexy as hell looking like a virgin in white.

She couldn't laugh because he was biting her and stroking her without going in, she could barely breathe, his big dick was throbbing and jumping against her ass.

"Baby, baby," he sung in her ear, this was when he put his finger in, his dick got even harder, her cave had become exactly what he created, his finger was soaked with her. He found her spot in no time, putting pressure on it and rubbing it too, making her orgasm inevitable.

"Lean back baby, you falling out, you alright?" he asked her, Mirah had almost lost her footing but he had a tight grip on her.

"Yes," she said out of breath.

"You sure?" he asked.

Mirah came and just leaned back until her stomach stopped convulsing.

He smiled in her ear, "That's round one, round two you going in my mouth, where do you want to meet at?"

Mirah gave him her number and took his, "before I go in for the night I'll call you," she laughed when she saw his name was Tyrone.

"Bet," he said as he pinched her ass.

She limped back to her seat. Mirah wanted a nap but the beat dropped for *I'm The Only One You Need*, and the crowd lost it again singing along with Mary.

"Girl what happened to you?" Lynette eyed her.

"This concert is the shit ain't it?" Mirah said and just started dancing.

Amtrak (Photoshoot)

"Misa? Is that you?" Pierre couldn't believe his eyes, Misa was right in front of him, in the tight hall way of the train headed up North.

"Oh Pierre, how are you?" Misa was just as surprised to see him, though she spent time talking on the phone with him regularly, she hadn't thought she would actually see him again and was very glad she had not texted him any naughty pictures of herself despite his constant begging.

Pierre was short for a man, he was about 5'6", he was light skinned with a low cut, his goatee was neatly trimmed and he was dressed in jeans and a thick Polo hooded sweater. Misa was much taller than Pierre, she was 5'8" in her ballerina shoes, her pants were tight around her hips and fell wide around her ankles, her shirt was an off the shoulder tri colored knit that showed off her matching bra. They couldn't stop smiling at each other.

"We never got up like we said that night," Pierre was talking about the last time he had came to town and invited her out to dinner.

"I know and now look," she smiled.

"Are you with someone here?" he asked her looking behind her.

"No I'm traveling alone," she replied.

"Where are you going?" he asked.

"Home and you?" she asked with a raised eyebrow, she knew he did a lot of traveling for work.

"Boston," he said.

"Really, I'm always talking about going there," she said wistfully.

"So come," he said.

"With you?" she asked shocked at the invitation.

"Yes," he said.

"Now?" she said still trying to make up her mind.

"Yes," he said again a little more direct.

"Yeah?" she stared at him in the face to see how serious he really was.

"Misa we can play catch up," he looked at her with a slight grin that made her blush.

"Where are you sitting?" she asked, her mind was made up.

"I have a sleeper, come on and get your things," he said and waited for her in the hall.

They went into the small compartment and had a seat. The conductor came by to announce that the diner was open.

"Good I've been waiting to eat," Misa was always hungry but her figure didn't show it.

They went to the diner to eat and talk, he ordered a bottle of wine and they drank it all and had to order another one. As they closed the diner, the couple staggered back to the sleeper laughing and copping feels off of each other, once inside the door he whispered in her ear, "Misa, Misa, Misa, I think about you all the time."

"We only talk on the phone a little," she blushed because they had been having phone sex for years.

"And like I said, I think about you a lot, but I do see

you on the web all the time but you refuse to give me an ass shot," he complained.

"What's better than the real thing?" she got up and bent over, "Ass shot like this?"

"Yes," he said.

"Ass shot like this?" she said and changed positions.

"Yes baby, like that, now take off something and pose for me," he sat down and pulled his dick out, despite his height he was really working with something.

"You see this?" he asked her. He pulled his Polo off and put it on the top bunk showing off his nice chest and abs. His dick was very thick, it seemed a lot bigger in his hands and on top of that he had the infamous curve in his shaft.

"Take that shirt off for me baby, but keep your back turned," he said as he continued to stroke his penis, "baby drop the shirt."

Misa crossed her arms and took her shirt from the bottom hem and raised it above her head holding it in the air, playing with it in her hands.

"Like this Pierre?" she asked.

Pierre gave good instructions and if she followed them closely it wouldn't be long before she was wet and her pussy was feeling a strong heart beat. He was a fashion photographer and specialized in bringing the sexy out of you. His voice seemed deeper in person but his commanding tone hadn't changed at all, Misa let go and let him control her with his words. She turned toward him, so that he could see how her breasts were barely held by her bra.

"Touch one baby, pull one out for me," she listened

to him and slowly brought it out using two fingers.

"Pinch your nipple for me baby," she bit her lip and he breathed out, "pull down your pants for me."

She did and raised her arms above her head, she knew this made her titties stand at attention. He continued to beat his meat as she stood there looking at his dick throb in his hand.

"Baby cock your leg up on the bed for me, rub the back of your leg with a finger and bring your other hand down to your pussy for me, she listened and began rubbing her pussy through her panties. She could see how hard his dick was and it made her mouth dry, or was it the wine? She didn't know and really didn't care, she wanted to stop posing and get that thing he was holding inside her.

"Baby, show me that pink thing inside your panties," she sat and leaned back on the bed and raised her legs up, she took her finger and used it to move the lips over so that he could see it.

"Baby it is so wet," he told her, "put your finger in it…now rub it for me, baby let me hear it." She knew what he meant, she would do that on the phone for him all the time. She made it wetter for him and then tapped it with her fingers a few times on the center of it. It was a slick sound, like a wet kiss, a real wet kiss. He was stroking himself a lot harder now.

"Put your finger in it again and bring it out real slow," she did it and then he came over to her, he made her very nervous yet excited because this was the first time Misa had actually been in his presence sexually, they were virtual lovers, sending pictures and such. But now he was here, standing over top of her.

"Do you want me to kiss it?' she asked.

"Not with this mouth," he said as he put his finger on her on her lips, it stayed there for a while until she opened her mouth up, "I want you to kiss my dick with the mouth of that pussy."

Her heart beat some more as he took the head of his penis and poked the hole with it. She tried to raise up and get it in further, but he used his hands and pulled back.

"Please baby, give me some," she moaned, he smiled, he knew she would be begging for the dick before it was all over. He took his thumb and rubbed her clit with it as he stuck his head in and out, it sounded so good to Misa, she just moaned, "oh yeah baby".

"You like this dick don't you?" he whispered this to her.

"You know I do," she breathed out heavily.

"Baby hold them titties for me, put them together for me," as soon as she grabbed them he went in a little further, when she licked her nipples for him and pinched them between her forefinger and middle finger he fell inside her, her back arched up and he kissed her neck, he hadn't stopped thumbing her pearl, so when he pinched it she screamed a little in his ear, he banged her out for that, he couldn't help it, plus he couldn't see her eyes any more, they had left when he put the head in the first time. He kept stroking her with his thumb and sliding that long dick inside her, the tip of his dick was constantly rubbing on her inner spot, it was like an overload because Misa had not stopped playing with her tits either. Pierre kept it up and made her feel the power of his dick by putting that curve all the way in and leaving it there. She couldn't breathe, the dick was taking all of her air away, she couldn't bounce back on it because it was too long, she had to wait for him to ease up on her and finally he did. He took his hand off of her clit and slowly brought out the dick from deep inside her, he fucked her with the head of his rod again with short fast strokes, again she tried to force it in further. Pierre gave her a little more but not much.

Misa was breathing faster and he could hear her climax coming as he moved her hands from her titties and took over for her. Misa came hard, he kept stroking it slow until she stopped. He took his dick out of her and started jerking it again he wanted to see his cum on her beautiful boobs.

"Misa? Baby I knew you had some good pussy girl, take a nap, I'll wake you up when we get to Boston."

Is He Furious?

"What am I going to do? Every time I think of him I have an orgasm," complained Taerah.

"I wish I had that problem," said Keshe rolling her eyes.

"No you don't. I'm standing in line, I cum. I'm at my desk, I cum. He calls me on the phone to ask me if I'm coming over, I cum before we hang up! It's terrible, I'm scared!"

"Are you for real? Just standing in line? What exactly does he do?" Keshe was very curious because she was between men.

"Whew it gets crazy. He's like a pussy maniac."

"Stop girl. I'm trying to drink something," Keshe laughed as her Cape Cod slid down her chin.

"I'm trying to be serious," Taerah continued, "he is so good, he's like a...I don't know, but it goes down in there. Like for instance last night he just attacked me on the steps, no warning. I came in the house. I barely got in the door. I had just locked it when he came running down the stairs. I jumped back because I thought he was going out the door. Well, no, he rushed me put his hand up my skirt and pulled my panties off! He took them, and smelled them while he fingered me!

My heart was racing from the onslaught, but then he

started
kissing me slow and deep till I was out of breath. His
dick was hard against my leg.

I always were lacy bras because he loves the way
my titties look underneath. Well last night I had
on a beige number, he unbuttoned my blouse and
went to town biting and licking me. The thing about
him is he rubs all three parts of the pussy when he's
on it, and it drives me crazy!

Anyway, next thing I knew he had given me a
thrashing up against the wall. I came three times! He
grinds on it, he bumps it, and I even caught him
pinching it. I have aftershocks for three days
minimum. After he came on my leg he told me to
wear panty hose tomorrow."

"I see you have some on," Keshe smirked.

"I know, and I hate myself for it, but shit what can I
do?" Taerah asked as she shuddered for the sixth time
that day.

Houseparty

House parties always had a sexual vibe to them. Not sure why, dim lights, music, and the scent of spicy foods. It wasn't surprising that Zelda found herself lusting after an unknown man. This party was going on, everyone was dancing, eating, and drinking. Zelda had found herself dancing with the mysterious man for a few songs.

Dancing with him was fun, he wasn't trying to feel her up, he was just doing his moves and Zelda was doing hers. His movements were fluid, he was about her height so when she turned around to give him the butt he just put his hand on her hip but left space between them. He broke away to get some air and smoke a cigarette.

She used the time to freshen up in the restroom. The bathroom was nice, pretty porcelain sink, with the dresser style cabinet. Looking in the medicine cabinet was considered rude, but it's a house party, so what could the host expect? Typical items, so that you could freshen up. But Zelda loved when people left personal items in there because it gave into their true personality.

"Wait a minute," Zelda said to herself, "I know this is not what I think it is... Yes it is.

"Wow," as she clicked the on switch she chuckled because it had working batteries. That was enough for

Zelda she had definitely gone too far, because she had an instant rush as her legs touched on her way to the door. She looked back at the cabinet and laughed again. Then she opened the door just as the mystery man was pushing it in. They had the same first step and it was directly into each other. After they looked into each other's eyes he pushed her back into the bathroom. He had seen that look when they were dancing and knew exactly what it meant.

Zelda was puzzled, because her pussy was already throbbing and to have this man push her backwards into a closed room and kiss her was a fantasy come true. Still this man she was kissing was nameless, beyond his stylish looks and his sexy body, who was he? Sadly that question would have to wait, because mystery man had found that wet spot in her panties and whispered in her ear, "is that for me?"

"Yes", Zelda replied in her sex kitten voice, "it is for you."

"Give me your finger", he told her, staring into her eyes.

She did and he put it in his mouth and wet the tip, mystery man had Zelda fingering her own pussy with his guidance. She was suppressing a moan from ecstasy when he asked her to show him that spot. She took him there with her hand, he told her to rub it soft for him, then he told her to just tap it a few times. He asked her could he kiss her pretty titties? She smiled.

"Unbutton your shirt for me sexy." Zelda let go of her pussy and began to unbutton the last 2 buttons on her four button blouse. Her nipples were very hard and her bra did very little to conceal that fact. She took the finger that she removed from pussy and

touched her bare nipples with it. He
told her thank you because he wanted to taste her
juicy pussy, and it got wetter because he decided to
lick Zelda's dark nipples.

"Take your heels off," he said, "and let's get in the
tub, we can pull the curtain closed."

"Put me against the tile," she replied, before Zelda
knew what happened both of her boobs were out and
up against the tile and her ass cheeks were being
lifted and spread.

"Baby, I want to fuck you with this long dick, can I
fuck you with it?"

"Yes baby, right there," she said forcefully.

Her pussy had a nice grip on his dick, and he caught
himself moaning as well. Just then someone came in,
he had forgotten to lock the door. The bath curtain
was completely closed, but Zelda's heels were on the
side of the tub. His mouth was pressed to her ear and
he told her to be quiet. She was breathing hard at first
so she lowered her breath and as she exhaled he filled
her pussy with a little more dick.

"Shush," he said but feeling his warm breath in her
ear, only made her more hot.

It was another woman in the bathroom, her perfume
was strong and sensual and her shoes clacked against
the tile when she entered. She used the bathroom and
when she flushed the toilet he thrust his penis in
Zelda hard and fast until the toilet stopped making a
loud noise. Home girl turned on the water to wash her
hands and did the same thing Zelda had done, she
looked in the medicine cabinet. She also took her
shoes off to see if Zelda's sling-backs fit, they didn't.
So she put her shoes on and left. As the door shut he

began to slide his dick in and out of her snatch. They were both moaning and breathing hard. He reached around Zelda and put two fingers on her pearl and rubbed it for her. Zelda felt the pressure and leaned forward, he placed his other hand on her breast and gently squeezed it rubbing the nipple with his palm.

"You like that baby?" He whispered. But before she could reply, the door creaked open again. This time a strong scent of cologne followed, it must have been Ralph Lauren Black because it made Zelda even hotter. The dude was on the phone, he lifted the seat up and flushed the toilet at the same time as he relieved himself. Zelda felt her lover pulled his penis out of her very fast and she thought he was going to ram it in her fast and hard like he did on the 1st flush, but she was wrong, he simply placed his dick on the rim of her ass and left it there, he gently rocked her back and forth on the tip of his dick. Dude using the bathroom looked down at the shoes and smirked, he had an idea of what was behind the bath curtain, but his cell phone rang again and the name that showed up meant that he had his own pussy plans. He walked out and left the door ajar.

Hater.

Zelda slid back a little, because the head of his penis was opening her ass up nice and slow, it felt good. He took his hands and placed them on her shoulders pulling her down on his dick, Zelda loved it. The head of his dick was making itself a warm wet hole. He kept at it for a while, "would you like a little more dick in your ass?"

He didn't wait for a response, he put his hand on her pussy, and told her to shut up, "this pussy is dripping down your legs, you want some more dick up in there".

Zelda slid back on more dick. "Your ass is tight, let me change that," he said.

He took a few steps back and pulled her with him. He took her head and nudged it down. Zelda's body was bent over.

"Beautiful," he said and he palmed the top of her ass as he banged it. Zelda couldn't keep quiet anymore, her moans got louder and louder. She had forgotten that the door was open and she told him to fuck her harder, he did. He had put more dick in her ass and Zelda was losing her balance. She slipped and he caught her around the waist with his forearm, "sit on that dick," he whispered in a raspy voice, "sit on that dick."

Zelda moved back on it and came. He felt her ass get tighter around his dick. He grabbed her titties and shoved his dick inside her all the way, exploding in her ass. He leaned sideways against the tile to catch his breath. Zelda got out of the tub, closed the door, and sat on the toilet. She looked at her legs and saw the slick clear liquid that had leaked out of her. He opened the curtain to come out and he was licking his fingers, "you have a sweet pussy girl." He went to the sink and washed his dick off. Zelda waited, and cleaned herself next. He was still rubbing his dick looking at her adjust her clothes.

Zelda looked at him and laughed, "baby I can't go again with you." She walked over to her shoes and tried to put them on. He laughed at her then because her legs wouldn't stop shaking long enough for her to get her toes in.

Decisions

Oh snap, that can't be him, Shema thought she had seen a ghost, was that him? Shema was driving down the street and had slowed down for a pedestrian, and from his walk it was definitely him. She couldn't remember his name, but she remembered how he made her feel that one afternoon of fun. Shema turned the corner to watch him walk a little more and drove past.

"Hey," he hollered.

Shema skirted to a stop, and stared through the rear view mirror to see him running up to her car.

"Shema?" he asked.

"Hey what's good?" she asked trying to sound nonchalant, just seeing him stirred up lustful memories.

"I hoped it was your car, I did remember you drove a Sterling," he said smiling.

"You saw my car?" she asked in disbelief.

"I walked you to your car," he told her.

"That's right you did, where you on your way to?" she asked him as she unlocked the door and he got in the car.

"Corner store and home, want to roll?" he asked her.

Shema looked at him, her eyes stared at his lips, and she thought to herself, how can you deny yourself an adventure like this. But she also remembered that she had a date with a real prospect in two hours. This situation, if she fell in, would definitely lead well into the night. So no, she would have to pass.

"Naw, I have to show two properties this afternoon, she paused for a few seconds, what's up with tomorrow?" she asked.

"That's good for me, call me in the morning," they pulled up in front of the store. He then leaned over to her and smelled her chin, "You smell nice, call me tomorrow," he looked at her pussy when he said it. Shema smiled so hard she had to laugh, "Trust me, I'm calling," she smiled and drove away. Her pussy was now throbbing because she knew he did not play. Last time he ate her pussy she came within three minutes. His skills were up like that, and she couldn't wait.

Shema got home and began to freshen up for her date, the event was black tie, so she decided to wear her peach silk gown. The bodice was shear with iridescent sequins and beads embroidered throughout. No underwear. The shoes would sparkle on her feet since they were beaded strap sandals. Make up would be light and natural and her long dreadlocked hair would be in a bun.

Her date arrived early so that they could have drinks first. His name was Derrick and he was as handsome as most Derricks tend to be. He was tall with dark skin and silky lashes. He even had a dimple in his chin. He had a baseball player's build, perfect proportions. They weren't having sex yet, but the sexual chemistry was there.

"How was your day today?" he asked as he took his first sip.

"It was cool, I ran into this guy I used to deal with,"

Shema said.

"Deal with how?" taking another sip.

"Oh nothing serious, but I was just thinking how small this city is," Shema took a sip of her drink and smiled at Derrick.

"Yeah, you run into everybody down here," he looked off laughing.

"What's so funny?" Shema asked him.

"Well my boy, the other day, ran into this chick he hadn't seen since their one night stand, and they got into a fight because she accused him of stealing her gold chain that night," he was cracking up.

Shema bussed out laughing, "Stop lying."

"I'm for real, shit like that always happens to him," he told her.

They finished their drinks and walked to the door.

"Baby you really look amazing, that dress fits your body perfectly," he said admiring her figure.

Shema smiled and gave him a kiss. They got inside the car and rode towards the gala. Inside the car Derrick kept tracing her leg through the split in her dress. Shema looked out the car window, trying to be as cool as possible. She knew this would have him drove. He kept right on touching her, and began playing with her nipple. He adjusted himself in his seat and continued driving. Shema noticed that her knees were no longer together and shut her legs. She also decided to close her mouth, because her lips had parted.

"Keep playing with me and I'm going to pull that thing out of your slacks, and I'm not swallowing so what would you do with the mess?" She looked at him out of the corner of her eye.

"Oh, you are going to swallow, my dick is going to be so far down your throat you will have no choice," he said looking her directly in the eyes.

"This I got to see, where is that dick going to be?" Shema took off her seat belt and turned her body towards him. She noticed how hard his dick was through his pants, and smiled at him.

"Don't smile at me," he told her. He put both his hands on the wheel, trying to steady himself. He had been imagining Shema licking and sucking his dick earlier that day. When she said she wouldn't swallow it made him think about one of those sloppy blowjobs where the woman lets the cum slide out of her mouth while she continues to stroke it up and out. Derrick wasn't sure if Shema was that freaky, but her lips were sexy as hell and he would definitely enjoy a mic check from her.

"Derrick?" Shema slipped her dress up.

"Do you want to see what you did to me?" Shema had slid her middle finger down on her pussy. There was a slick shine on her finger. "How am I going to walk around with slippery goo running down my leg?"

Derrick pulled the car over and turned it off. "Hit the hazard lights," he instructed as he opened his door and slowly walked around to her side of the car.

"No Derrick," Shema protested, "No I'm scared of outside sex, I am loud!"

"I am not going to fuck you, I'm just going to clean you up real fast," he said in a soft matter of fact voice. Shema turned toward the passenger door of the car with her legs open and her feet on the street. Derrick kneeled down in front of her, resting his knees on the

36

doorframe.

"I'm just going to clean you up real fast, take your finger and show me where that mess is," he said in his deep Barry White voice. Shema took her middle finger and went up and down.

"Put that finger down there again for me," he instructed in the same throaty voice.

Shema did and on her up stroke up she felt his tongue following behind her finger, she moaned.

"This will be fast baby, real fast," but he said it very slow as he slid his finger inside her. Then he spread his tongue over her fat lipped pussy. His tongue was a little bit longer than her pussy lips and that worked to his advantage. She moaned loudly and that made his dick harder. He put some more pressure on the top of Shema's pussy and sucked the clit in between his teeth, flicking it with his tongue hard and fast. He didn't let go even though Shema squirmed. Her moaning became harder and harder.

He knew she was about to pop. So he took the clit from between his teeth and pressed his tongue on it with warm gentle force. Her pussy gave way, and he sucked all cum up until it was clean. Derrick got up and smiled at Shema.

"Turn the hazard lights off," and he walked back to the driver's seat. Shema could barely move, but she did her best to reach over and hit the button she then pulled her dress back down and leaned back to put her seat belt on.

Derrick looked over at his sexy date and smiled again, he thought to himself about the dude Shema ran into today, I have to lock this one down quick, he said to himself.

Shema looked over and smiled too, that orgasm was in less than two minutes, looks like I will not be making that call tomorrow.

Housewarming

Kiera was on her way to her cousin Tiera's house. Her cousin had recently moved back to the old neighborhood and was trying to get back into the mix. The new house was cute, as Kiera rode up she could already tell that her cousin stayed there, the porch was completely decorated. The patio set was a cherry toned wicker, the planters were turquoise and filled with thick leaved plants, the cushions on the chairs were crispy linen white, and her straw shades to enclose the porch were cherry red as well. Tiera's favorite spot in any home had always been the porch and the bathroom and Kiera could not wait to see that room.

As Kiera walked up the stairs Tiera was coming out of the door, "Hey Kierr," she smiled and hugged her cousin.

"Aye Ti-Baby," Kiera said laughing, "no one calls me that but you, how do you like your house?"

"I love it, wait until you see the kitchen, it is so live, the cabinets are so nice," she said directing her cousin through the home showing her all of the rooms. After the tour they sat down in the kitchen to have a drink.

"Do you want some iced tea, it is spiked with peach vodka?" Tiera asked as she brought two glasses out of the cabinet.

"Of course I do", Kiera replied, "now tell me about the guy you met."

"Oh yeah let me tell you, dude is so funny, he had me cracking up today, but let me take you back to the beginning," Tiera said as she put ice in the glasses and poured the tea.

"Yes, start from the top and don't leave anything out," Kiera smiled.

Tiera sat down with her drink and passed her cousin's hers and began her tale.

"Okay so I got here about two months ago and like the first night I called my girl Jackie from college to come over so we could smoke, so she gets here and I pull out my stash and we get to rolling up, after she took a few pulls she was like ill where did you get this shit from, so I told her dumb ass off real quick and she told me that the weed man with that fire was right on my block. Now I saw a bunch of dudes out earlier on the porch two houses down and across the street, sure enough that was the house. She called him up and told him to come through, at first I was like damn girl I don't want these dudes around here up in my business, but girl when I saw him I was like damn, and he was like damn too. So we all chilled in the crib at first and we just talked, found out he is an investment banker with his own Internet Company."

Kiera interrupted, "he told you all that?"

"Hell no I googled him while we were talking," Tiera was laughing out loud, "if he was showboating I would have been like ill, but anyway yeah girl, he came over the next night to check on me and when I answered the door I wasn't really dressed, I had on my house shorts and a tank top.

Kiera interrupted again, "No bra either, huh?"

"Kierr you know how I am," she laughed some

more, "but anyway stop interrupting, let me tell you while I am still in the mood to share, so I invite him in and he is looking so good, he had on a pair of jogging pants and I could see his dick print girl, he's like 6'3" and milky brown, I was so happy I was indecent for him to see. Girl he comes in and we sit down, I was sitting on the floor going through my music before he came, so he starts checking out my collection down on the floor with me, I had no furniture yet, only the porch was done. We went hip-hop first of course, he likes jazz so we listened to a little of that, I played some exclusive shit to him that I got from grandpop. I go get some wine and come back, he found some R&B while I was away so we started vibing to that, and that's how it began. Girl he put on Silk, *There's a Meeting in my Bedroom*, you know what that song can do, so yeah he starts to caress my leg and he's just chilling rubbing my leg, I'm like damn his hands feel so good and he's just on my outer thigh, no further, so while he is touching me I felt myself getting hotter and hotter, he noticed too and when he did he like smacked my ass and kept rubbing my legs up to my ass, every now and again he would smack me in the same spot. Every time he did it I felt myself throbbing, he got up and brought me out side to sit on the porch, I was glad because I needed some air. Well he pulls down the shades and turned off the porch light so basically we are in the dark. He sits me on his lap and starts rubbing on my legs again, this time he is inside my thigh and girl my shit kept spreading for his ass. His touch was so nice to me because it was gentle and forceful if that makes sense."

"Hell yeah girl, I know that feeling, you were just melting on him weren't you?" Kiera asked taking along sip of her drink.

"Yes I was, I had leaned back onto him and he moved my shorts over and played around my panties for a minute, I was embarrassed because I know they were soaking wet. He just rubbed on the lips as soft as he was on my leg. He kissed my neck as he played with my pussy lines, I was done, I was getting so worked up I almost took his hands from him and went left. But no, luckily I had a little self-control because what he wanted to do I could only imagine and I was going to let his ass lead. So he starts fingering me with one finger, he's going in and out and then he would come all the way out and played with whole pussy just rubbing on it with his whole hand, never had no shit like that before, I just laid back with my legs spread open and he kept making me squirm. He pulled my breast out of the shirt and began fondling them and every few pokes inside my pussy he would pinch my nipple, girl I was so ready to get that dick in me I was getting aggressive. He laughed at me and told me he had something for me if I act good. Girl I straightened up real quick and just relaxed against him he started to kiss on my neck and next thing I knew I felt his penis going inside me. His dick fit perfectly inside me, he settled me back and made sure it was completely in and then he started to rock me on it. He asked me if that was the spot I liked, I was silent because I had zoned out, he laughed in my ear and told me I had a nice tight pussy. You know how you have a dick inside and your pussy tightens up around the dick and it is really like a glove? A wet glove? Well yeah that's what was going on. He was on me from the back so between my titties and my pussy his hands were taking turns. I was losing it but I kept rocking on his dick. He said baby I want you to come for me, can you do that, can you make that pussy jump wet for me? His voice was fucking hypnotic, I was like yes, yes I can come for you, he was like do you need me to beat on the pussy like this, girl he had lifted me up by my waist and started to beat on it so fast but not hard, he must have felt the spot I liked when he had me fucking his dick the way I liked it, 'cause girl he found it and set it off. He slowed the pace down for a little while and made me get all hot and bothered again. I knew then that he loved to play games cause he wanted me to get aggressive again so I did. I rose up on him and closed my legs and girl I started to crash down on his dick like I was smashing cans with my feet, he was breathing real hard and had let my pussy go all together, he had my titties in his hand and as I came down on him he twisted my nipples. I was screaming oh yeah baby louder and louder, girl he had to bite me on my ear and whisper to me to keep it down. I landed on him and opened up my legs for him he picked up where he left off and he started to touch all my buttons right, needless to say he was ready for me to blast off so he hopped in my ear and told me he liked the way I take dick, that my pussy was so slippery and wet, and that he wanted me to come with him. Girl he started banging on my pussy again and I know I was about to skeet he asked me where to put the cum I told him let me catch it, girl that shit sent him and he pounded my pussy up in the air again and he picked me up off of him to suck on his dick while he came, Girl my box emptied out on me and I made a mess right there on my porch. I had a rug out there but after that episode I rolled it up.

"Stop playing, you got some good juug right down the block?" Kiera screamed.

"Yes indeed and so far so good," Tiera told her with a big grin.

"Are you guys exclusive yet?" Kiera asked.

"No not really, he saw me going out on a date the other night, he came over soon as I came home acting all curious. I just laughed at him, I figure he'll lay down the law as soon as he can't take it anymore," Tiera giggled.

"And if not?" Kiera inquired.

"Then I will enjoy it while it lasts, can't hate the player, can only hate the game," and Tiera finished off the last of her drink.

Ms. Thea

A little plump was a good way to describe her, she was only a biscuit away from being fat. Her curves were still in place. She wore a pink and grey workout suit to show off her efforts of trying to stay fit. At forty-nine she considered herself a sexy woman.

Ms.Thea had never gone inside a sex store before. Why she was sitting in her car contemplating entry was too funny. Thea Wells had been single for years, and her bitchiness had become the family joke. At the last gathering a few of her nieces suggested she make a trip to Spring Street to see what she had been missing. After she cursed them out and let them know all about themselves, including their inability to get a descent father for their many children, she left out in a huff.

Two days later Thea was downtown in Philly on Spring Street, nervous as she watched two young women walk in the adult store, an older gentleman with his too young girlfriend, and one obvious transvestite. Thea wondered if she wanted to be amongst their ranks. What did they get that she didn't? Fuck it, she told herself, putting change in the meter she walked in. She had expected a sleazy environment with the smell of stale cigarettes and cheap musk. Pleasantly surprised, she found a very clean and orderly establishment. The first thing that caught her eye was the movie posters: The Cosby Show with Misty Stone as Denise, The Jeffersons,

Good Times, and a triple X SoulTrain. Oh this is too much, thought Thea, but she found herself a little aroused just walking through the collection of DVDs. Then there was the wall of dildos and other devices. Ms. Thea was floored when she wandered over to the anal section.

"What the fuck is an anal douche?" She asked out loud. She looked around but no one had heard or paid her any attention. Thea continued to look at the many beads and rings but found her way back over to the lady toys.

The young woman that had come in with the much older man came over as Thea picked up an Eager Beaver.

"Not to be all in your business, but, if that isn't a gag gift don't waste your money," the young woman said.

"Gag gift, what's that?" Thea screwed her face.

"No nothing like that," the girl smiled as she explained, "I just know from experience that those don't get the job done."

"Well, what would?" asked Thea.

The young woman gave her the same thing she was getting, a clear vibrator with three speeds and a clitoral stimulator. The price was $89. Thea had no idea if this was a bargain or not. She just walked to the register and paid.

As she left out of the store the older gentleman that she had seen come in earlier with the young girl was leaning against the wall. He was a little older than Thea. Dressed casually in some dark corduroys, a cashmere sweater, and a Kangol that matched his soft leather shoes, he was very handsome. He caught her eye, and passed her his business card. Earl Hammond.

"Call me and I'll show you how to use it," he said. Thea wanted to tell him a thing or two, but decided against it. She did need help, and maybe a random man was what she needed too.

"Drop your uh, niece off, and I'll call you in an hour," she told him.

The old man almost dropped the cigarette from his mouth as he made a beeline back into the store to hurry his little friend along.

Thea got home and took a sensual bath, creamed her body, and made the phone call.

"Hello," the man said.

"Hello," she said back.

"Hey baby, what part of town are you in?" he asked.

"Parkside," she told him as she walked around her huge house placing odds and ends back into their place.

"Okay, I'm on Bradley Street, how do I get to you?" he asked.

Thea gave him directions and waited at the door. He walked up the steps smiling. As she opened the door, she awkwardly smiled back. He came in and looked around her home, it was immaculate. The L-shaped couch caught his attention first and he moved towards it. Thea was still at the door not knowing what to do next. There was nothing to fix, so she slowly walked towards him.

"Where's the new toy?" he asked.

"Right here," she handed it to him.

They sat on the couch and he opened it up from the box.

"Go wash it off first. Rinse it real good for me," he instructed. Thea did as instructed and returned.

"Okay baby I need to ask you a few questions," he started.

"Oh, I didn't want to get to know you, I just wanted some help," Thea said cutting him off.

"The questions aren't about you baby, I want to know about your pussy," he said.

"Oh," she said feeling stupid.

"I need to know if you like to come clitorally or internally," he said.

"You sound like a doctor and I really don't know the difference," she said.

"All right then we'll find out together and I'm going to show you the difference. Lift up your négligée for me and pass me those batteries," he told her.

Thea did as she was told. She passed him the batteries first but hesitated on easing up her nighty.

"Baby, I'm not going to hurt you. I want to make sure you feel really good, trust me," he pushed the button, hitting each knob to make sure they worked, but settled on the 1st level.

"Are you sure that's going to be enough?" Thea thought out loud.

"Let's see, I have to get it wet down there before we start," he was staring at her and smiling as he said it.

"You have beautiful taste in lingerie," he said as he rubbed the top of her lace panties and traced her pantyline with his finger. Placing the device on her pussy lips he lightly followed the length of them and then rested the vibrating tip on her clit.

"Do you like that baby?" He asked. Thea was staring at him and didn't respond, he took that as a yes and applied a little more pressure. He then went back to tracing her pussy lips because his only mission was to have her begging for more.

"Can I take your sexy panties off? I want to watch that pussy get wet," he said.

She stalled a bit not knowing how to be seductive. She began to remove them but he beat her to the punch. Rubbing the small of her back, he slid his warm hands inside of her satin panties and cupped her ass. She was surprised at how good it felt to have her ass touched like that.

"Your skin is so soft," he told her. Thea did take great care of her body.

He continued to rub her ass because he knew it would loosen up her sweet juices.

Thea found herself more aroused, and began lifting her hips up so that his hands could get more of her ass. Easing her panties off very slowly, he put them to his nose and inhaled. Thea laughed and called him a, "freaky man."

"Yes I am," he replied, "and I love good pussy. Let me see what we have down here." He separated her knees for her because they had clamped shut when she laughed. Slowly, her thighs began to separate and he watched as the darkness between her knees gave way. Her pussy lay open with a hot pink line and a slippery pearl ball. The ball just needed to be poked and a silver stream would fall.

"Beautiful," he said as he looked at her, "let me see this a little more closely."

Luckily the couch was roomy and shaped with space for two, he was able to positioned himself on his stomach with his face between Thea's thighs.

Taking the toy he began to trace her lips with a little pressure, and Thea spread a little more for him.

"See baby, always remember it's the pressure to get the juices flowing." He continued with the lips for a while, and then he placed the tip of the toy on the little pearl. The pussy started to move before his eyes, so he put it in a little further. "Thea," he said, "there's a little spot inside you that feels really good when it's tapped, take the toy from me and find it."

Thea opened her eyes in surprise, "I thought you knew where it was."

"I know what to do when you find it, now take it out my hand, and show me where the spot is."

She was very hot and excited and she slowly took the vibrator and slid it in deeper. She was surprised at how smooth the entry was. Her helper had made sure she was too wet to feel any discomfort. As she moved it in, she felt a slight tingle when she passed a certain spot. Then she felt it a bit stronger.

"I think that's it," she said, "I like it right there."

"Okay, give it back to me sweetness. He took the toy from her, turned it on the second notch and mimicked her movements with his other hand on the top of her pussy. Clit and all, he began massaging it. Thea began to breath harder.

"This pussy needs attention baby," and he fixed in on her rhythm, "take one of those titties out for me. Let me see one." Thea did as told.

"Pretty titties to match your pretty pussy, ain't that right?" he said, "now pinch on that nipple for me," he demanded.

She did so, and began to moan.

"Baby I think you're coming for me, pinch those

titties, pinch them for me!" he demanded.

Thea clenched up and the man noticed, "let go baby, loosen that pussy for me. Let me see your pussy skeet out for me."

Thea moaned, "ohhh, I'm ohhh." He poked her quick on that spot and pulled the device out of her pussy. As it came out so did her juices.

"Ohhhhhh," Thea moaned slower.

"That was the internal orgasm," he said as he continued to rub her pussy. Thea was catching her breath and smiling real hard.

"Now, I want to show you the other one. Give me a few minutewith this device right here," he said as he placed his index and middle fingers on her swollen clitoris, and turned it back down to notch one. "Is that all right with you?" he asked.

Thea laid back further on the couch, and bent her legs up so that access was easier.

"I guess the answer is yes," the man said, and he put the device on it with long strokes. Then, he set it on the clit and rubbed it back and forth making it pop a little. Taking his finger, he set it on her pussy. Thea was jerking forward with his touches. She clenched again and almost did a sit-up. He shoved his fingers to her spot and tapped on it. His finger got wet and warm as she came. Swirling his finger inside like a magic wand, all of the cum Thea had made came out with his finger. It was a clear sticky mess. He held her pussy juice up for her to see.

"What do you want me to do with it?" he asked. Thea was staring in awe at what had just happened. Thea didn't move, she continued to lay back.

He came up to her mouth with his finger, "I just

want you to see what kind of mess you put on me with this good pussy of yours."

When he left he got to the door and turned to look at Thea. "Now look, don't go out into the world like that anymore. When I saw you earlier it was written all over your face. What you want to do is wake up a little earlier every morning, and put yourself to bed a little earlier each evening. You will know when to put it down for a while. Be easy sexy." And with that he rolled out in his shiny Cadillac.

Weeks passed, and Thea got real familiar with her toy. She spent many free days getting new batteries. The next family event was coming up, so she went to the store and bought each of her nieces a copy of Steve Harvey's book *Think Like a Man, Act Like a Lady*, she figured she should pay it forward.

The Juke Joint

Tracy and Sidney had been trying to find something to do ever since they arrived in Judah, Mississippi. They were staying with Sydney's Aunt Bibi in her small shotgun house. Bibi was old-fashioned in her ways. While she allowed the un-married couple to spend the night under the same roof, she would not allow them to share the same bed.

Sydney's cell phone rang, and they both began to laugh. His ring tone was Kevin Hart's *Alright, Alright, Alright, You Gonna Learn Today*. It was his cousin Sammy.

"What's up?" said Sidney.

"We're on our way over to pick you up, be there in an hour," said Sammy. Sammy always had a plan, even though he lived in a small town, he knew everywhere to be.

Sydney hung up and looked at Tracy, "We have an hour to get ready."

"Do they know I'm coming?" she asked.

"It doesn't matter," he said brushing the question off, "what are you going to wear?" he asked.

"Jeans, a tank, a jacket, and my heels," she replied.

"Heels? In the country baby?" he said.

"Heels anywhere, I'm good," she replied.

"All right hot girl," he laughed at her. He loved the way she dressed, no matter where they went she was always the flyest chick in the building. Her hair was braided up in a mohawk and that alone would have all eyes on her.

The two got ready and sat on the porch drinking hard lemonade, waiting for his cousin. As it got later and later, they got more and more drunk. Aunt Bibi came out on the porch to check on them. She gave them a few citronella candles to keep the mosquitoes away. She also had a glass of their lemonade before she went to bed. Sidney finally showed up at about 12:30 AM. They laughed at each other as they stumbled, trying to get up and walk to the car. The car was packed with Sammy's three boys from college, with only one seat available. They had come to visit from Atlanta on their way to New Orleans.

"Aw man, I'm sorry, I didn't know Tracy was rolling with us man," Sammy said. He didn't know how they rolled as a couple, but that wasn't his problem.

"That's all right," Sydney told him, "she can sit on my lap."

"Cool," he said, "let's go."

They rolled out listening to *Goodie Mob* and Tracy found it funny that the song *What You Niggas Know About the Dirty South* was playing as they arrived at their destination. It was a barn, set back in a field. Cars were parked all over in no particular order, and music was coming from cars and the barn. They decided to parking lot pimp for a little bit, so Sammy opened his trunk and pulled out his gallon of Ciroc with some little red cups. Sammy was notorious for being cheap. He actually had 4 ounce cups to pass around, and he added juice to everyone's drink, a lot of juice. His friends were cool and didn't seem to care. John was an engineer who traveled a lot, Richie was a veterinarian that specialized in livestock, and Dutch was a consultant of some sort, no one was really sure. They all stood around the back of the car listening to music and drinking.

"Man, I want mine straight," said Sidney.

"Then you might want to talk to a bartender," said Sammy.

"Look at this shit man," Sydney held his cup up to the stars, "this is all juice, I can't get a double shot cousin?"

"You free to go order what you want with a bartender," Sammy replied.

"Tracy don't drink this shit, I'll get you a real drink," but as he spoke Tracy was already downing her drink. "Damn baby, I wanted to pour the liquor out in front of him, you know?"

"I couldn't Sid, I refuse to waste alcohol," she laughed and gave Sammy her little cup, "can I get a refill cousin?" Sammy was livid. He wanted to take her cup from here and put it back in his trunk, but instead he gave her a straight shot.

After laughing at Sammy and his cheap ass, they made their way into the barn. Tracy could not believe her eyes as she walked in. There was a live orgy going on. Men and women, women and women. The bartender was even getting his dick sucked as he made the house drink. Sydney slid his hand around her back and led her to a corner. He knew his baby would not participate, but he also knew her to be a serious voyeur.

The club was decorated in a rustic look. The tables

were light ash wood sanded down to smoothness. The floor matched in color, but had a high shine and huge plush throw rugs scattered throughout. The bar was old-fashioned, but modernized by lights under the counter with different colored bulbs. All of the liquor was in mason jars with a spigot, and the orange juice and lemonade were freshly made. The juke joint smelled good, earthy wood and fresh fruit. It was almost hard to smell all the sex in the room.

Tracy noticed this one girl sitting backwards on a stool with her back facing a tall man. Her ass was completely off of the seat and he had clear access to her pussy. Watching him whisper in her ear was erotic. He pressed his fingers into her hips and lifted her up slightly to pull her down harder on his long dick. Tracy could see his dick swelling by the vein, and the woman's juices made his dick shine. Tracy watched the woman bounce back and forth. At one point the couple made a puddle. As the woman slumped over the stools back, the guy whispered in her ear again, she straightened up suddenly. Putting her foot back on the rail, she started to bounce again, until he fucked her off the stool again. Tracy felt a slight throb and put her knees together. Sidney kissed her neck and asked if she wanted another drink. He knew the answer and went to the bar.

Over on one of the plush rugs were three women. A Dark Skinned Cutie was having a good time sucking loudly on one of her partner's shaved pussy. Her mouth nuzzled her mound and you could see her tongue lapping on the lips every now and then. Her partner was a pretty Caramel Lady with perky titties that had the darkest little nipples Tracy had ever seen.

Her pussy eater snaked her hand up to one of those dark nipples, and begin to twist and pull. The third woman, another Chocolate Honey, was on her knees in the middle of the two. Her tits were huge and real. Ms. Caramel had three fingers hidden inside her dark pussy, her hand moved in and out slowly, and each time it came all the way out she would pat it with her fingers. The Dark Skinned Cutie was now fingering her own pussy as she sucked and licked on her friend. The Chocolate Honey was moving her waist around in little circles as her wet pussy was being played with. Her big boobs were moving from side to side in circles. She fell over in a doggy style position, and Ms. Caramel caught one in her mouth. The pussy eater looked up and saw them. She stopped sucking the pussy to play with her own. As soon as she stopped sucking, Chocolate Honey placed her hand on Ms. Caramel's pussy and gently rubbed it. It seemed like all of them were about to cum.

Tracy spotted an odd couple over by the bar watching the threesome reach its height. An older, short man and a tall, thin woman in her early 20s. He was on a stool and she was standing up next to him. As they watched, she pulled his dick out of his jeans and stroked his long penis up and down. He pulled one of her tits out of her tube top and began sucking on it. This went on for a while, and though they were both basically fully clothed, it was very erotic. He began to squeeze her thighs and inch up her skirt, little by little until a bare pierced pussy was revealed. He continued to suck her titties and squeeze her nice ass. She took his thick dick and hit it on her leg. Then she changed her position to play with her pierced clit.

He never stopped sucking, licking, and squeezing her pretty tits.

Sydney looked up and saw that Tracy had a big smile on her face. He held back a laugh. Instead of asking what was so amusing, he followed the direction of her eyes only to see his cousin Sammy having his dick sucked by two women. They were each taking turns. He was leaning back against the wall with one of his little red cups. The first one bobbed her head on his dick really fast. The second woman licked the bottom of his balls while waiting for her chance to send him over the edge. The first girl used her hand as she choked and sucked on Sammy. She took it all the way in and gagged, releasing the dick for her teammate. Her friend in turn traveled from his sack up to the tip of his dick, and slowly descended down the shaft with his stick inside her mouth. His tool disappeared in her mouth, and her tongue clipped the top of his balls a few times. Sammy leaned against the wall even harder. The first woman waited patiently behind her partner, rubbing her tits and smacking her wet pussy. Sammy caught sight of her and almost spilled his drink. She seemed like she couldn't wait to have his big dick in her mouth again, and when it was her turn she approached his dick differently. Placing both hands on his dick, one above the other, she smiled up at him and put her tongue to the head of his tool while massaging his dick. Tracy was learning a thing or two from these women. She was gonna practice this on Sidney tomorrow.

The woman took long licks, and continued to slowly suck his dick. On one of the up strokes, she took the tip of her tongue and circled the head of his dick really fast. When she and her partner spit on his dick, his big dick spit back at them. Sammy spilled his drink as he fell back against the wall. Grabbing his dick away from his friends, he milked the rest of his cum with his hand. Sammy looked as weak and helpless as a newly hatched baby chicken. Sydney and Tracy laughed out loud because they knew Sammy would be mad that he wasted his liquor.

First Time For Everything

It was Shauna's first time working as a call girl. She had several friends who were doing really well for themselves, and each swore their weekly visit to the Ritz-Carlton's Bar and Lounge had them on top of things.

"Shauna it's easy, all you do is have a seat at the bar," Darniece told her, "you already have the look, just go be yourself and come home a lot richer."

"Are you crazy? What happens next?" asked Shauna.

"Trust me, it all takes place in one space. The men that come there already know what time it is, so you sit and wait for a bit. You make sure you look approachable and beautiful. They start by paying for drinks, I usually just stick to wine at the bar. I will babysit the first glass to see what he might want. If he's tossing them back, I'll toss them back too. You kind of follow their lead with the drinking, you know?" Darniece explained further and it began to make perfect sense to Shauna.

Shauna and Darniece arrived at the Ritz at about 7 PM, right after happy hour so the cheap drinks and the men who wanted them would have already left. They each ordered a drink and began chatting. As they laughed, a nice-looking man walked up and sat down a few seats away. Darniece sent him a drink. He smiled, and came over to them. Shauna noticed his build, 6'2" and fit, not overly muscular, but the cuts were definitely in place. His shoes were expensive. His shirt was Burberry. His watch was foreign-made, and in his ear was a small black diamond stud, squared at the edges. Handsome. Shauna had decided she would leave with him for free. Darniece could tell, and brought the conversation in the correct direction before Shauna turned their spizot into a dive.

"So what does your evening look like?" he said as he smiled away from her.

"That would depend on you," said Darniece.

"How is that?" he asked.

"What would you like my evening to look like?" she smiled.

He smiled even harder, and Darniece blushed back, he's sold. He slid money to the bartender, and began paying for their drinks. They talked some more and he began to describe how he and Darniece could spend the evening alone in his room. He told her about the view of the city from his balcony, and how if he had his way, they could see it together in the morning. Darniece knew what that meant. She whispered in his ear her donation amount. He okayed it, and they left Shauna sitting at the bar nursing her drink.

Shauna was alone for a few minutes at the bar when her cell phone rang in a text message. While she read, she hadn't noticed the sweet man that had approached and sat in her friend's absent seat. She checked his eyes first, they were a clear, beautiful amber and his smile was unnerving. Shauna could see why her friends enjoyed this high living. These men were so attractive.

The point that Darneice pushed the hardest was to be friendly and conversational so that you appeared to be old friends to any onlooker. Shauna had that part down. She knew how to get along with anybody. He looked Shauna up and down and asked her if she came here often.

Shauna laughed and told him he must have a better line than that.

He laughed at that and gave her a shy smile, "well, have we met before, you look familiar?" Shauna laughed even harder.

"Next you're going to tell me that you don't do this often," Shauna said.

"Or maybe, did you hurt yourself on that fall from heaven," he laughed.

"That's a good one," she told him, "as long as you didn't tell me that I should be tired from running through your mind all night. They both laughed.

Shauna felt at ease looking into his face, though she still couldn't understand why a man like this would have to pay for it.

"My name is Sincere, can I get you another drink?" he asked motioning the bartender to come over.

"I'll have another Chardonnay please," the bartender took his card and returned with her drink.

"You aren't having one Sincere?" she asked as she finished off her glass and pushed it to the edge of the bar.

"I actually don't drink much, I smoke a lot though," Shauna was looking into his eyes and didn't notice any tell tale signs.

Their conversation moved easily. She was sipping

the last her drink as he motioned to the bartender again.

"Oh, no thanks," she said, "I've taken the edge off, I'm ready to relax and take these shoes off."

Sincere looked down at her shoes, they were nice, soft Italian leather. They didn't look like they hurt at all.

"Well in that case would you like to come to my suite for a bit?" his smile was all she could see, but she remembered Darniece's instructions on the donation fund. She mentioned the amount to him and he didn't flinch, he just grabbed her hand, and led her to the elevators.

Shauna went into his room and they immediately began to touch each other. He touched the swell of her breasts with his long fingers. Then, taking his hand away, he licked his thumb to play with Shauna's nipple. Shauna closed her eyes.

"Are you enjoying my touch?" he asked.

"Yes," she replied.

"Tell me," he demanded.

"Yes, I love your touch," she breathed heavily.

"Where would you like my next touch?" he asked.

"Down there," Shauna pointed.

"Show it to me," he said in a low voice.

Shauna took a few steps back. She began to unwrap her burgundy silk dress, as it fell he looked at her magnificent body. Shauna wore no panties or bra, all she wore were the garters to her thigh high pantyhose, and high heels. Sincere loved it.

"Show me where you want me to touch you," he said again.

Shauna leaned back against the wall and began to

caress herself for him. He watched her please herself, noting how she rubbed her pussy with such gentleness, and how she touched her nipples after she cupped her breasts.

He walked over to her and began to take over. Kissing her neck, he pressed against her, glad that she had left her heels on because she was a lot shorter than him. He pressed her up against the wall, and as his hand cradled her wetness he continued to kiss and lick her neck.

Shawna had so many apprehensions about her first time, she couldn't believe she was breathing so hard nor how much she was enjoying herself. He noticed the smile on her face, and kissed her chin line and brought her nipple up to his mouth. His breath was sweet and warm, and his light kisses had Shauna weak. She was putting more of her pressure on his hand, and Sincere was loving the warm glaze that was making his fingers wet. When he stuck a finger inside of her, Shawna let out a whimper.

Sincere eased off a little, leading her to the bed. He motioned for her to get on top of it.

"Put your knees together and get doggy style for me," he instructed.

Shauna did as he said, she raised up on her hands and knees while he sat behind her caressing her round ass. His hands swept back and forth on Shauna and she began to arch her back for him, giving him a nice view of her pussy as it got even wetter. Sincere placed two fingers at the top of her clit and gently rubbed it with a little pressure. Shauna's arch got deeper. Sincere's fingers spread away from each other and trailed her damp pussy back and forth. As he moved his finger, he applied a little more pressure and Shauna's breathing changed. She was so turned on she tried to spread her legs open.

"Put your knees back together," he said in a low demanding tone. Shauna did so immediately. Sincere took his two fingers and squeezed the lips of Shauna's pussy until he saw the clear gel slide out between her lips. He then rubbed the wet line he created.

"You want me to drop some dick in you?" he asked Shauna.

"Yes," she said, "drop some dick in me."

Sincere raised up from his seated position and got behind her. He unzipped his pants and nudged her knees open. Putting his weight on Shauna's back, he put his cock inside her very slowly. "Pretty pussy baby."

Shauna felt his heat as he pressed into her. His dick was thick, long, and warm. She loved feeling his dick slide in the length of her. It was even better when he pressed her back in with his hands to deepen her arch. Shauna looked back at Sincere in disbelief. His stroke was so right. She started to pump back, picking up speed as he smacked her ass. He told her, "keep that pussy still," and she held it in place as he pumped the spot deep inside her really hard. Shauna moaned.

"Place your head on the mattress baby," he said sweetly. Slowly Shauna followed his command, and got facedown, ass up. Sincere rubbed her back with his long fingers all the way down to her ass. Then he picked it up a little as he slid in her wet pussy. She moaned louder. Sincere got up off of his knees with his dick still deep inside her he put both his feet on the mattress. His hands were on her ass at the very top pressing down.

Shauna moaned again, "baby, drop that dick in me," and Sincere did. In a furious style he fucked her as hard as he could, and she loved it. Shauna kept moaning, "drop that dick in me." Faster and faster she said it, and harder and harder he pumped.

"Ahh," Sincere screamed out as he pulled out his dick and let his cum shoot out on her back. "Can I write my name on your back?" he asked.

"For more money you can do whatever you want," Sincere laughed and wrote his name with his cum on her backside. Shauna laughed with him, until he stuck his dick back inside.

Shawna couldn't believe how fun her first time as a call girl was. She didn't expect to have one of the best fucks of her life. Just as Shauna was thinking about it, Sincere was sucking and licking on her neck. He had slowed down his tempo, and was now rubbing her titties. Shauna was back on all fours trying to maintain, but with the pressure it was becoming too hard. Sincere raised up again and put his hand on the crease of her thigh. His penis was still hard and he banged Shauna's pussy with a swiftness. She fell to her belly on his last thrust. Sincere knew he was wearing her little sexy as out. She was trying hard to take the dick, so he was going to reward her with a nice orgasm. Shauna was on her stomach with her legs slightly open.

He whispered in her ear, "close your legs, I want to feel some tight pussy."

She followed his instructions and he in turn sunk low inside her. "Sexy baby," he called, "do me a favor?" He didn't wait for a response because he knew she was feeling his long dick deep inside her pussy. He had found a wall and was rubbing it right.

"Take your hand and play with your clit for me."

Shauna took her hand and quickly found the spot he wanted her to press. She began to rub herself with his rhythm, "how does it feel baby?"

"I'm about to cum," she informed him in a tight clipped voice.

"Let it out baby. Rub that pussy for me," his tone was so seductive. "You take nice dick baby." As he rode her from behind, he felt her breast again and began to play with her nipples. She moaned out again, as his fingers went at her nipples, twisting and turning them like knobs. Shauna was still playing with her clit and she began to tense up. Sincere knew she was close to letting go. He thrust his cock in to help. Her hands sped up as she rubbed, and Sincere continued to play with her tits. Shauna came hard and as soon as she stopped shaking he pounded that spot so hard that she came again. He kissed her neck and told her he wasn't done yet. He banged her, and Shawna buzzed again. "Give me one more baby," he said. After she tightened up and went limp, he banged it again and this time Shauna felt herself leaking out onto her fingers.

He climbed off of her and moved up to Shauna's head. His Dick was shiny with Shauna's cum.

"Can you lick it off for me sexy?" he asked her so sweetly.

Shauna rolled to her side and looked up at Sincere, "can you feed it to me?"

Sincere put his stick in his hand and leaned toward her. Shauna opened her mouth wide and attacked his dick with a vengeance. His dick was too big for her throat. In her attempt to deep throat only half could go in before she gagged and had a saliva trail from her mouth to his dick. She did it again but this time she grabbed a hold of his balls and gently cupped them.

He grabbed her head and told her, "I'm going to fuck your mouth. Don't put your teeth on me."

She simply opened wide and relaxed her jaw.

Sincere fucked her mouth and swiftly pumped it, "Poke your tongue out, I want to cum in your mouth."

Shauna slid her tongue out over her teeth and waited, Sincere was still pounding away. Shauna saw his dick swell up, causing her to gag again as all of his little soldiers spilled out into her mouth and down her tongue. She licked the head of his dick as he continued to nut. Slowly she licked and sucked until it was all out of him. Her hands were still wet from her own juices.

Sincere took her hand and licked her finger, "sweet pussy," he said to her as she smiled back.

They laid there a while together, both exhausted. Shauna was the first to move, she went to the bathroom to freshen up and get dressed. When she returned, he was fast asleep in the bed. She simply walked out of the hotel room, richer than when she entered.

The Classy Dame

It started out like most mornings, trying to decide what to wear, cream lace bra with the rose straps, French-cut lace panties with the pretty rose bows, beige A-line skirt that fits just a little too tight, a gold silk blouse just sheer enough to see my brassiere, and now for the shoes, cream sling-backs or my sexy reptiles? The sling-backs it is because it won't be a long day.

My man and I have decided to fulfill our fantasy tonight, we used a chat site to find an appropriate partner for our threesome. We finally met the kind of woman that turns both of us on. A classy dame so to speak. The meeting place was decided, a nice lounge downtown near the federal building. I knew I would be running late, giving them a chance to vibe without me, and I love to watch my man from afar. I like to see the type of women that catch his eye. They tend to range from petite to medium-small, pert little boobies to big round melons, and always a nice ass. That happens to be one of his specialties. So I stood over by the bar for a minute. I had a good view of him, his chocolate brown slacks, and lemon custard raw silk pullover. I couldn't see his shoes, but I knew they were Cole Hans. I could see her too, and it made me happy to know I chose the sling-backs while she chose the pumps, something like a precursor to the evening. She had legs for days, long and slender. Her hands were well manicured, and I could just imagine how my baby's stick would fit between those nice fingers. I had told him that I wanted a little help with that dick, so we began surfing the web to find something spectacular.

I watched them interact a little before I came over with my drink in hand. My man smiled and stood up. He laughed when he saw my wine glass because he had already ordered me a drink. She rose and laughed with us, saying how she would have to catch up with me.

We sat and spoke easily about the going-ons of the news, crazy people at the checkout line, and why transvestites always work in adult stores. I had to admit she was so sexy. When she stood up I noticed her height. Just to watch her move while in conversation was just so sexy. Her blouse was buttoned in a way that whenever she laughed her nipple would show through underneath her bra. Her lips were inviting, I kept visualizing her lips sucking my baby's dick. At one point she noticed me staring at her lips, and stuck her tongue out as she picked up her drink. Just a little tongue between her teeth. She asked if we could go over to her house because she didn't live that far. We agreed and drove our car. During the ride my man asked me what I thought of her. I told him she's like my twin. He felt the same way and told me he wasn't sure if he could handle two of me. We laughed and I placed my hand on his dick and told him, "you know I need help." It got hard immediately.

We pulled into her garage and followed her inside. The living room was very cozy, and good music came from the stereo. She came back with three wine glasses. My man and I sat on the love seat and began to kiss. He felt my breasts through my shirt, placed his hand on my neck and caressed it. She came over to us and placed her hands on both of us, rubbing my legs first. Somehow she made her way up to my breasts and scooped one out and into her mouth. My baby slid his hand up my skirt and rubbed my pussy through my panties.

"Baby your pussy is so wet," he said.

"Let me taste it," she said, and she helped raise my skirt, moving my wet panties over. Her tongue traced my split and my clit, "this pussy is so wet."

We stayed like that for a while, just enjoying the sensations. My man watched how slowly she sucked on my pussy, making low kissing sounds. I took notice of the hand job she was giving him, his dick was really stiff in between her fingers, so big and black that it looked like silk. She began to jerk it faster.

His arms were wrapped around me as he played with my nipples. She kissed my pussy one last time before placing my man's dick into her mouth. Her titties finally made an appearance. They bounced with her as she bobbed. I asked her to take it all the way down. Slowly moaning, she took that dick all the way down her throat. I had been right about her lips, they looked so good sucking my baby's stick.

Then, she pulled me toward her. I raised up to meet her on my knees. Making my way to the base of his dick, I licked and sucked. Her lips were next to mine and when she came down she put my tit in her hand.

My man was enjoying her but he told me to get on his dick and suck that candy out. I did it of course, but she wanted some too, so she started to kiss me right on the head of my man's penis. I put her two nipples between my fingers and with a little pressure she moaned her way down his dick again.

My man now wanted to play with my pussy, but first he wanted to see it. He loved my box. I sat on the couch with my back against the arm. I opened my legs so that he could watch me play with my pussy. Home chick was gagging on his dick, and came off his head with strings. The look in his eyes made both of us do it again. She gagged again while I pulled my fingers in and out of my pussy. I reached over to him and put my finger in his mouth.

While sucking him, she grabbed my pussy real tight. I moaned. Home chick put her finger inside me, pulling a little juice out, she put it on the shaft of his dick. I then touched her pussy only to find it dripping down her legs. Looking at her, I smiled as she said she loved sucking dick. I wanted my baby to feel how wet her pussy got from putting his nice dick down her throat, so I helped her raise up and straddle his dick. She slid down on his dick, moaning again. I got behind her and put her nice full breasts in my hand as she rode his dick. My baby loved it!

She was so turned on by the two of us toying with her, that she rose up off his dick and got on her feet so that she could come down hard. I went to kiss my baby and he put me on top of him in front of her. He began pinching, twisting, and pulling my nipples. He knew that drove me crazy!

Homegirl began kissing my back and my neck as she rode my baby. He saw me slowly losing it and he knew it was time for some penetration, so stuck his finger in my pussy. I lifted up a little and he brought his hand up to our new friend's face.

"Taste my baby's sweet pussy," he told her as she stuck her tongue out.
"Yeah, this is that good shit," she started to cum, and my baby pounded her up a little more.

I got off and sat on the back of the couch. My back was now against the wall and my man turned around so he could eat my pussy. Homegirl got down under him and started to suck his dick again. It was an erotic scene to see, her on the floor playing with her pussy, sucking dick, my man with his nose and chin all in my pussy. My baby wanted me to cum, so he started to talk to me about how good his dick felt. She was gagging and spitting on his dick and he was licking and sucking on me between words. He opened his whole tongue on my pussy and it was that lick that made me burst. My cum on the tip of his tongue made him reach his peak.

She asked me if she could she catch it all. I let her and told my baby to make it slow and get it down her throat. She moaned again and started to cum. He missed her mouth because she jerked with her orgasm and it landed on her cheek and chin.

We were all spent and sat staring at each other in amazement. She got up and went to the bathroom. When she came back to the living room, she had a bottle of wine. Pouring each of us a glass she sat down. We talked about a few comedy routines that made us laugh, and set a date to hit up a club in the area that had local comedians on Tuesday night. Then she invited us to her bathroom where there was a huge whirlpool bathtub. I brought the bottle of wine and she brought the glasses. We all climbed in and got comfortable. The lights were dimmed and the water was scented with a soft musk. She told us that this wasn't her first threesome, but it was by far her most enjoyable.

Can I Speak to Mike?

Ring! Ring! Ring! Stephanie looked for her cell phone under her pillow. She had gone to bed early last night because her son was going on a school field trip the next day, and if she missed the 6:40 am bus she would have to make a three-hour drive to DC.

Ring! Ring! Ring! Who could this be? It's like 3:30 in the morning. Stephanie found the phone and answered, "Hello?"

"Yeah," a deep voice answered, "I have your ankles up by your ears right now and I'm giving you some long slow strokes in that good pussy of yours," click, and the phone call ended.

Stephanie took a long breath mainly in shock that Michael would call her and talk to her like that just to hang up. She couldn't go back to sleep. In fact, she was quite awake now, imagining the long strokes he described. "My ankles by his ears?" she said out loud, "my goodness. He plays too much." She laughed and pulled a cigarette out of the pack on her nightstand.

Michael and Stephanie had not actually had sex, and beyond their sexual foreplay on the phone, she had no idea what it would be like. Stephanie knew he wouldn't call back again tonight, so she put out her cigarette and reached for her device. She knew how to have a good time by herself, and decided an orgasm would help put her back to sleep. But Michael was paying for this one, "had me up smoking cigarettes in my bed," she thought again out loud.

The morning went well. Her son made it to the bus on time and saved Stephanie $120 in gas, so she was in a great mood. Right after she walked in the door her phone rang. It was Michael.

"You were wrong for that Mike," Stephanie answered with a laugh.

"Baby, I thought about you all night. I had to call you," he told her.

"You got me all hot in the middle of the night," she said.

"I wanted you to feel like me," he said to her.

"Well you won, I had to relieve myself."

"Oh yeah?" he asked. "Tell me about it, what did you do?"

Stephanie went to her bedroom and began taking off her clothes.

"Tell you about what?" she asked Michael back.

"What did you do to that pussy," he asked.

"I rubbed it."

"With what," he encouraged.

"My hand first."

"Your hand, or your fingers?"

"My fingers actually."

"How many?"

"Three."

"Which three?"

"My index, my middle finger, and my ring finger."

"Which did you use to plug it?"

"My middle and my ring."

"I thought so."

"How do you think so?" she asked.

"When I imagine you touching yourself, that's how

I see it," he told her

"Oh interesting."

"Why?" he questioned

"You imagine how I play with my pussy?" she asked.

"Yes I do. Like now, what kind of panties do you have on?"

"None, I just took them off, but they were lavender, and lace,"

"Lavender?"

"Yes, and there was a little bow above my ass."

"A present for me?"

"Of course."

"Can I hear how that pussy sounds?"

"What do you mean?" she had no idea how to make it sound off.

"Do it for me, put the phone down there so that I can hear it, tap on it"

Stephanie placed the phone between her legs and began to pat her pussy with her fingers. Surprisingly she was wet. She didn't know how she got that wet, but after tapping there was no question. She placed the phone back to her ear.

"Did you hear that?" she asked slowly and seductively.

"No, put it back down there."

"If I heard that, I know you did too."

"That thing sounds like it feels so good."

"I like it too, now my fingers are all sticky."

"Is that bad?"

"Yes."

"Take everything off."

Stephanie took off her bra and began rubbing her

breasts with one hand, squeezing them and moaning.

"Stephanie? Are you playing with your pussy?"

"No, I'm squeezing my breasts."

"Tell me about your titties Stephanie, are they big?"

"No, medium."

"Are your nipples big?"

"Yes."

"Like what?"

"Like beaux dollars. Just very dark, my nipples are very dark."

"Do you have a natural hang or do they sit up?"

"They sit up by themselves. They would just fit in your mouth if I sat on your lap."

"If you were on my lap, what would you do?"

"First I would position myself just right so that I could feel that bulge on my ass. I would rock back and forth for a little bit to make it harder. Then I would turn toward you and place my titties in your mouth. I'd put one in your mouth at a time, and then I would place both of them in there. I would whisper in your ear, and tell you to touch my wetness for me. Just touch it."

"Are you still rubbing your breasts for me Steph?" he asked in a raspy voice.

"Yes I am, I have the nipples between my knuckles and I'm pressing it. It feels really good."

"Could you touch your pussy again for me?"

"Yes baby," Stephanie put the phone back between her legs and tapped the wet spot repeatedly. "Feels good," she moaned out. She stuck her 2 fingers inside and the phone fell out of her hand. It hit the pillow, slid to the floor, and crashed into pieces on the hardwood floor. "Pay backs a bitch," she said as she continued to please herself.

Married Men, The Sad Affair

"It's not going to take long, pullover," Yancy asked her friend Hansa.

"No, because it's hot out here and you like to leave people in their car," Hansa said back.

"Just pull over, I'm not going to stay. I just have to pick something up," Yancy pleaded.

"Yeah, I know, I'm not stopping. You can check dude out own your own time," Hansa said squarely.

"That's messed up. If I have to come back across town for five minutes," Yancy said with major irritation.

"You know good and well it won't be five minutes," Hansa responded.

"Yes it will, please pull over," she begged again.

"I'll let you out, but I'm gone. Get back to work in a cab." Hansa looked at Yancy and smiled.

"You're so messed up," Yancy looked away pissed.

"No you are," Hansa followed up. "Last time you had me late and sweaty, sorry chicky chick. You got me once and you know my motto, first time…"

"Last time," Yancy finished her sentence.

"That's right, see, you know me," Hansa said as she giggled to herself.

Yancy rolled her eyes. They were on their lunch break and she wanted to stop by her man's house to get a few dollars. But Yancy knew her friend was right, it was never just a minute when she was with him.

"Don't roll your eyes at me," Hansa laughed.

"Look, whatever, let's just get back to work so you won't be late," Yancy let her words draw out slowly.

They rolled in silence until Michel'le's song came on, and they both began to sing *Something In My Heart*. Pulling up to the lawyers office that Yancy's father owned, they both got out.

Hansa handed Yancy a $100 bill, "you're good 'til we get paid," she told her.

Yancy took the cash and put it in her purse as she walked up the stairs into the building. Hansa walked into her office and left the door open, and Yancy followed behind her and shut the door.

"Thanks for holding me down," said Yancy.

"I know you got a problem when it comes to him. I had an addiction before, you remember?" asked Hansa.

"Oh yeah, girl, you had it bad," Yancy shook her head in remembrance.

"I know, and if it wasn't for him having a secret life I would still be in that shit."

"Well *my* love affair is not shit. He's actually a good guy," said Yancy indignantly.

"But he's married," Hansa said looking at her friend with concern.

"Separated," she retorted.

"Married is married," Hansa reminded her.

"Look, if she's not in the same city, they are definitely separated," said Yancy calmly.

"How long has this been?" Hansa inquired.

"I'm not getting into all that, just give me the Whitfield file, I got work to do," she said.

Yancy left out the office with a smirk and a pep in

her step. Hansa smiled after her and opened her own file up.

Yancy sat in her own office and started working on her portion of the Whitfield file when her phone rang, the caller ID read Big Bank and she smiled.

"Hello," said Yancy.

"Hey baby, what happened, I thought you were coming by to pick something up?" asked Big Bank aka Gerome.

"No, I had to get back here and do something," she told him.

"Do you want to come by my place tonight?" he asked.

"I can't, I have to work. I had this afternoon free," she said.

"Oh maybe this weekend then?" he asked.
"Yeah, I'll see you Friday night. Want to meet me at d.b.a.?" she asked.

"Yeah, I'll be there a little after work," he said, "call me on your drive home."

"Okay, I will, see you baby," said Yancy.

She hung up the phone and smiled some more, thinking about what she'd wear, perhaps the wide legs and the silk scarf as a shirt.

Hansa

Hansa sat at her desk looking at a memo she found on her desk when she returned from lunch, "meet me in the stacks." She knew what that meant, and smiled to herself. It had been five years since this affair started and it was still just as exciting as the first day. She finished up her work for the day and put all of her folders in order. Grabbing her clipboard, she headed towards the office library in the attic. Yancy had just left and the office was empty. The reception area was clear of the three paralegal students, so she climbed the stairs of the old Victorian house finding a note on the first landing, "Take off your shoes." On the second landing, "take down your hair." And a note on a portrait, "take off your skirt." Hansa grabbed each note and did everything they told her to do.

Yancy

Yancy was driving home at this point while talking on her phone, smiling ear to ear.

"We would have these parties and everyone would dance, not one wallflower," he told her.

"What, who was the DJ?" she asked.

"The same cat that runs the d.b.a.," he said.

"Stop playing, they're always jamming in there," she said.

"That's why, do you want to go tonight instead of Friday?" he asked.

"Yeah?" Yancy was surprised at how quickly the tables had turned.

"Come on," he said in his sexy voice. She hesitated for a moment.

"Okay, I'm on my way," she said.

"Me too," he told her. "Hey, did you eat yet?"

"Yeah", she said. "Did you?"

"Not really."

"I got you," she told him and hung up the phone.

"Shit," Yancy thought out loud, "he's going to give it to me tonight."

Hansa

Hansa stood in the doorway of the library wearing her glasses, a silk blouse, and pantyhose with wild hair falling at her shoulder. Benjamin stood by a bookshelf staring at her. She walked over to him, and he put his hand up to her mouth. Her lips opened slightly while his finger grazed them. Her tongue slipped out, he kissed her. Her heart was pounding in her chest. He looked so good to her. His body was slim and firm, even though he was 58-years-old. His frame was slightly chiseled, and his suit fit perfectly. He smelled fresh with a spicy richness, and his beard was flawlessly trimmed. Hansa took her hand and began rubbing his chest through his cotton button down. Benjamin's shirt felt so soft and smooth, she could feel his hair beneath the shirt. Damn this man was fine, and she felt her snatch box getting wet. Benjamin put a key in her hand.

"What's this?" she asked.

"Keys to your new office," he told her.

"Benjamin, you did it?" she said.

He didn't answer. He went down on his knees. Placing his palm on her ass as he moved the hose down with his other hand. He gently patted her ass with his open hand. Hansa felt his breath on her lower lips. It was warm, strong, and deep. He left the hose down by her feet, and she stepped out of one foot. Benjamin took his finger and opened up her lips, rubbing the middle with his first two fingers, he felt her sticky wetness. Then he rose to his feet and turned Hansa around so that her back faced him. He reached in front of her and put his same two fingers on her snatch, rubbing inside.

"Say you want it Hansa," he whispered in her ear.

"I need it now," she could barely breathe.

He put his fingers on her pearl and pressed down before he started rubbing again.

"I want some dick Benjamin, now." She let a forceful moan escape her mouth.

He unzipped his pants and pulled his dick out, placing it right between her pussy lips. Hansa put her hand under his dick and began to rock back and forth.

"Slip it in please," she breathed.

"Take my titties out," he told her.

She let go of his cock, and quickly unbuttoned her blouse and clipped her bra open from the front. She rocked back and forth on his dick with her hand underneath, letting it slide out as she came forward. She pushed his dick inside her, and fell forward so that she could get some leverage.

Yancy

Sitting in the car staring at Gerome, Yancy fought back the urge to take his dick out and kiss on it. Why did he have to wear jogging pants, she wondered to herself.

"Yancy, do you eat Greek food?" he asked.

"Not really, but I love their salads," she told him.

"Good, I know this place uptown, you'll like it," he said.

Yancy was looking at his pants and it was making her horny. He pulled into a dark gravel parking lot. There were a lot of trees surrounding the back of the restaurant, with only two cars including their own.

As soon as he parked Yancy grabbed at his pants, pulling out his dick.

"I can't wait Gerome," she said, and she began to kiss wet and slow around the head. Leaning back in his seat, he stared at her slowly taking his dick to the back of her throat. Yancy came back up to the top and started bobbing on it.

"Damn girl," he said as he pulled her hair out of her face.

"Do you want me to stop?" she asked.

"No baby, no," he breathed heavily and Yancy continued. She sucked on his head and slowly slid her tongue out of her mouth, resting the bottom of her tongue on the tip of his head. She then applied some suction, and she bobbed up and down some more.

"Suck my dick baby," he told her and Yancy did. He was loving the tenderness of Yancy's tongue.

Hansa

Hansa was taking long slow strokes in her pussy. Benjamin hadn't stopped slowly rubbing on her clitoris with his two fingers. She was so wet, and she was breathing so hard. She raised up on her toes and came down on her heels.

"Oh, you want to be fucked?" Benjamin steadied himself. Pulling his fingers away from her pearl, he rested both hands on her hips. Spreading his fingers out, he pulled her into him. There was a slapping sound that took over the library. Hansa was coming back with a lot of force, but she wanted him in deeper, so she moved her hands from the shelf and used them to spread her ass open for Benjamin.

"Oh," she moaned as he banged her harder, and she

almost fell.

"Touch your toes for me," and he bent her back, "touch them so I can get at that wet pussy."

"Benjamin I'm cumin," he pulled his dick back and let his rim hit hers. Faster and faster he pushed it in. Then he shoved it all the way in until he hit a wall. She moaned again. Faster and faster he popped it. Benjamin put both her boobs in his hands and used them to pull her down further on his dick. She had never had a man grab at her mounds in order to fuck her harder.

Yancy

Yancy was in the parking lot having the same luck. Her mouth was being fucked back by Gerome.

"Just stick your tongue out for me. Let me run my dick on it for you."

She felt so good. Her mind was racing behind the tingles in her pussy. Why does it feel good to me too, she wondered. He was gently stroking her mouth and letting his dick rub against her lips.

"Kiss my john again," he told her and she applied more suction, not letting up.

"Where do you want it?" he asked her. She swirled her tongue around his thing fast, popping it out with a snapping sound. Popping and sucking up the saliva that had spilled out, his nut was about to come out. His dick got harder and she forced her jaw to release some more.

"Ahh, that's so good," Yancy had his dick between her lips and let it hit her. She sucked it out nice and slow and his dick stayed hard.

Yancy lifted her skirt around her waist and

straddled him. She took her hand and guided it inside. She went down low on him so that her pussy rubbed against his hair.

"Yance," he tried to talk but couldn't. She didn't move her body at all. She rested her chin on his shoulder and relaxed her walls around his dick while kissing his neck. She then ran her tongue over his bottom lip, and gently forced it into his mouth. Yancy felt his big rod throbbing inside of her. That's what she was waiting for. She wanted him to feel her tight, wet pussy for real, so she continued to kiss him slowly while rubbing the back of his neck. His dick jerked inside her again, and tapped a nice spot deep inside her. He felt it too. He stopped kissing her and wet his thumb. Taking it down to her clitoris, he flicked on it gently. Yancy began breathing heavily. He continued to pulse inside her as he flicked. The motion between them was so subtle. They were both caught up and close to climaxing. Gerome hadn't stopped flicking her, and his dick hadn't stop jerking on the walls of her pussy. He took his other hand and placed his fingers on her lips. She opened her mouth.

"I want you to suck this dick too," he told her, putting his middle finger in her mouth.

She followed his instructions and felt her pussy contracting, so did he.

Gerome let out a deep moan, "suck that dick baby." He put his finger further down her throat, and her pussy contracted again. He applied more pressure on her clit. Yancy felt him, and pressed toward his thumb, making a slight rock up and down.

He felt her pussy jumping wet, "suck it some more," he told her as he put his finger in and out of her mouth. He felt her orgasm welling up and let his big dick jerk faster.

Yancy moaned out. He put both hands on her waist and rose her up so that he could bang the last bit of juice out of her. Yancey slumped over him and went limp.

He rubbed her back, "you really can fuck your ass off Yancy."

She laughed but couldn't move. "Baby, what was that? I came so hard," she said.

"You swole that dick up," he told her.

"That's what happens when that dick gets big?" she asked.

"Stop talking to me before we get a ticket," he said.

"What?" Yancy asked.

"Yeah, they call this a crime against nature, and I don't want my picture in Just Busted. Now get this good pussy off of me," he told her.

Hansa

Hansa was on the floor of the library leaning against the shelf still trying to recover her breath. Benjamin sat between her legs.

"Benjamin, what did you do with my titties," she asked.

"I used them to hold onto you," he told her.

"That felt so good, like they were made for that," she said.

"I'll show you something else later, if you want," he smiled at her from the side and she kissed him on the back of his neck.

"What are you going to do about your wife?" she asked him.

"What do you want me to do about her?" he asked.

"What men usually do when they fall in love with someone else," she replied.

"Hansa, you're 28 years old, I'm 58 years old. Do you really want to take care of an old man?" he asked.

"Stop that Benjamin, you know how I feel about you, and you keep coming to me. You just bought me a building," she said with her voice raised.

"I like things like this Hansa. You're so sexy and smart, you work all the time, you don't date, so you don't know what else is out there for you," he told her.

"I get out, so I know what's going on out there. I just want you," she told him.

"You want me to leave my wife? Yancy's mom? And then what?" he asked her.

"I'm in love with you," she said.

"I won't leave Yancy's mother," he told her.

"You have a hickey on your neck," she said as she stared miserably straight ahead.

Yancy

Yancy was back in the passenger seat using the mirror to reapply her lipgloss.

"Are you still hungry?" he asked.

"I'm too tired to sit in a restaurant right now," she told him.

"You want to go back to my place?" he asked.

"I want a glass of wine, and some good music," she told him.

"Let's go to d.b.a. then. Maybe one of the food trucks are out," he said.

"Let's get some wings out in front of Club

Caribbean," he suggested, he straightened his jogging pants, put the car in reverse, and headed downtown.

Yancy's cell phone rang, "Hello Hansa. What's up? You want to come to DBA?"

"I keep falling in love with the wrong men," she said.

"Why are you crying?" Yancy asked.

"Because I'm in love with a married man that won't leave his wife," she said.

"Hansa, they never leave their wives, we all know that," she replied.

"But his wife doesn't even care about him, she doesn't even want him," she said.

"How do you know? There's always two sides to a marriage story," her friend told her as softly as possible.

"I know because he's been with me! I want him so bad Yancy," she said.

"I didn't know you were this far gone with him. I tried to mind my business on this one but shit, he's my dad!" she said.

"You know?" Hansa asked.

"Everyone in the office knows, hell, my mom knows," Yancy told her.

"She does? How?" Hansa questioned.

"They've been married for years. She just stopped acting out, but she knows," Yancy said.

"I feel so stupid, he won't even consider leaving," she said.

"He's almost 60. He can't keep up with you," Yancy told her.

"That's what he said," she replied.

"Hansa, you're my girl and I love you, but shit,

everyone knows you don't mess with married men. That's my dad and that's how he moves. You grew up with me, remember when we were freshmen and the drama during Spring Break?"

"Don't remind me," Hansa said.

"But you need to think about that shit, you were there."

"I wanted him back then," she told her friend.

"How do you think that made my mom feel? I know you don't want to think about her, but she had to hurt knowing you were the new chick," she said.

"He just bought me a building for my own practice," Hansa said.

"And he'll give you anything else that you want, but you have to play your part," her best friend said.

"My part?" Hansa didn't like where this was going.

"Yeah, your part, stop trippin," Yancy said to her.

"Yancy, I'm hanging up."

"Do that, and stop crying, where are you?" she asked her.

"In the stacks."

"First things first, get away from the crime scene and go home. I'm on my way over there," Yancy said.

Big Banks' eyes bucked, "What do you mean? This was our date night."

Yancy looked up at him and hung up the phone.

"How are you going to just drop me like that?" he asked her.

Yancy sent a text to her father, "you play too much with women."

"Is she really fucking with your dad?" he asked her.

"Yeah, for years now, about five."

"How do you deal with that?" he asked her.

"I'm a lawyer, and I'm his daughter," Yancy called the China Tea Garden, "I'd like a delivery at 2933 Burgundy: one shrimp egg foo young, one order of crab rangoon, vegetable lo mein, one order of fried chicken wings, four shrimp rolls, and two shrimp balls."

"Will you call me so I can take you to your car?" he asked her.

"No, but I will call you when she falls asleep. We have some unfinished business you know, are you going to file for your divorce?" she asked him.

His cell phone rang and he answered.

Yancy smirked, and enjoyed the ride all the way to her best friend's house.

Coming Soon From
Thynkupp Publishing

To The Dogs

By Nicollette Gonadu

A story of a young girl that arrives in New Orleans during the famed era of legalized prostitution. Thelma starts out as a lowly house girl for two wealthy madams and becomes the proprietor of the best brothel in the city known for its exotic beauties with the skills to match. Heartbreak doesn't find this woman as she moves through all of the echelons of the city's underworld, her country girl charm leaves men vying for a place in her life, any place that she may allow them to fit in. As the city changes so does her style in supplying the one thing that the city cannot get enough of.

Coming Soon From
Thynkupp Publishing

Expert Advice

By Nicollette Gonadu

Meet Lori Ayers, relationship counselor and urban activist for the hood. It has never been hard for her to give therapy to her loved ones, in fact she had been the confidant to the grown women in her neighborhood since the early age of ten. Lori had a come a long way from her dorm room as free counselor to coeds, she was now a counselor to the stars. Between keeping her marriage intact and managing her family's dysfunction her career takes off, but will the highlife jeopardize all that she has acquired on her climb to the top.